Nailed: A Blue Collar Bad Boys Book

Blue Collar Bad Boys, Volume 2

Brill Harper

Published by Brill Harper, 2017.

This is a work of fiction. Similarities to real people, places, or events are entirely coincidental.

NAILED: A BLUE COLLAR BAD BOYS BOOK

First edition. June 8, 2017.

Copyright © 2017 Brill Harper.

ISBN: 979-8223291800

Written by Brill Harper.

This story includes a bonus epilogue that was previously only available by signing up for the newsletter. Have fun!

About this Book

Brody

I'M NOT THE KIND OF guy you leave alone in your house. I'm especially not the kind you leave alone with your innocent daughter.

My newest client doesn't seem to care. He just wants his office remodeled.

His college-aged daughter isn't my usual type, but under those prim clothes and too big glasses, the sweet little bookworm hides a tight little body that's tempting AF.

I make her nervous. I should. I'm going to make her mine.

She doesn't know about men yet...

She's about to learn.

Megan

Dad's carpenter makes me feel things I don't understand.

I don't have any experience with older guys like him, or any guys really. They look at me and see a quiet nerd. But this bad boy—I feel like he sees right through me.

Like he knows the dirty fantasies that haunt my dreams. The things I do under the covers. He makes me needy and breathless.

But I'm shy and awkward—what do I have to offer a man like him?

AUTHOR'S CONFESSION: This book is super sweet, unfailingly filthy, and the heroine is nerdilicious. And who doesn't love a bad boy who's good with his hands? Very good with his hands. Very, very good. Brody is the Alphamallow you've been waiting for. If you like opposites attract, other side of the track, bad boy/good girl romances with instalove and over the top feelz, you're in the right place.

CHAPTER ONE

Megan

When the carpenter knocked on the door, I was expecting someone else. I mean, I knew a carpenter was coming, I just didn't expect someone like *him*. I figured someone older. But Brody Maines isn't old. He's older than my nineteen years, but probably only by five or so.

I'm holding my ginormous science textbook in front of me like a shield. Not that it could help much—neither the book itself nor the knowledge inside can help me now.

I'm over my head.

Brody is a big man—he has to be over six-feet-tall by three or four inches, and his muscles look like they are currently trying to tear out of his t-shirt. From a scientific perspective, which is usually my only perspective, he's an excellent specimen of the male species. His waist-to-chest ratio affirms the correct V shape to indicate a higher level of testosterone and correlating dominance. His square jaw and ridged brow also indicate that he is likely in high demand as a mating partner.

While my knowledge of biology is strong, it is not helping me communicate at this moment. I am better with books than people. But the books are right when it comes to sexual selection. I want to have this man's babies just by looking at him.

We stand in the doorway, me on one side, him on the other, an awkward silence filling the space between. Instead of forming actual words, all I can do is blink up at him.

Way, way up.

He is all man in a way an inexperienced girl like me, even with my lack of people skills, knows is trouble. He radiates power and a kind of dominance that makes me weak in the knees. I feel overpowered by his presence, but I *want* to be overpowered. It is quite disconcerting.

His eyes are gray, no that's not right. They're too dark to be called gray. Maybe charcoal is a better description. And they are focused on me.

I really should be saying something. Like "hello" or "come in."

But I get sidetracked by his hair. It's thick and a color that's not blond, but not brown either. It appears to be silky soft. It occurs to me that I've never touched another person's hair. In all the years I've been alive—that can't be right, can it?

Yes, I suppose it is.

My father is not affectionate with me. Or perhaps I am not affectionate with my father. I love him. But we're not close that way. And I have never been the slumber party kind of girl, so no hair braiding with my friends. And well, my lack of hair touching opportunities with boys in high school was not a surprise to me or the boys I went to school with.

College has turned out no differently at this point.

I'm just an odd girl. I always have been. I'm too serious. Too studious. And too introverted to break out of that mold now.

So if Brody's hair looks silky soft to me, I don't have prior experience to base that on. It's just a hypothesis.

I have a lot of those. Unanswered suppositions.

His eyebrows are drawing together like he's confused. Which is my fault because I'm handling answering the door in a very weird way. Trust that I can take any situation and turn it into something awkward. It's a gift.

His cheek bones are sharp, his nose a little crooked, but his lips make my insides flutter. The bottom one is plumper than the top, and it makes me want to bite it. Since I've never bitten anyone before, nor had the urge to, I don't know why it feels like instinct.

Bringing my gaze down, it lands on his hands. They are massive. They look so strong. Like he could crush things with them, but I know, instead, he uses them to create things. Beautiful things. My dad, who is by nature a collector of beautiful things, hired Brody to put a built-in desk in his office like the one he saw at his friend's home office. My dad didn't care how much it cost. He didn't even try to negotiate. That is unusual. Not his competition to one up his friend—that's normal for my dad. It's the not negotiating a price down part that is off his normal baseline behavior. He must really want that desk. I saw pictures of some of Brody's pieces, and he is an artist with a good reputation for his work.

I bet he has a bad reputation though, too. I can't stop thinking about how his rough fingers would feel on my untouched skin. I'm getting wet and it's embarrassing. This getting wet thing is a bit new to me as I've only started recently. Delayed onset of sexuality has hindered my ability to fit in with my peers for years. And now that it's here, I don't have anyone to talk to about it. People my age have been dealing with this for a long time. It would be strange for me to approach someone about it anyway.

Brody looks at me like I'm a wild animal he's trying to coax out of a trap. He puts his hands in front of him so I can see them. He inclines his head to look less aggressive. "You're Megan, right? Did your dad forget to tell you I was coming? I can wait out here while you call him."

"Uh." *Speak, Megan. Speak.* I'm just dumbstruck. Which is ironic considering my brains are really my only asset.

"You okay?" His jaw squares like he's clenching it, and he looks beyond my shoulder into the house. "Are you afraid of me or is something else scaring you? Is someone in your house?"

Before I can tell him nothing is wrong but my inability to act like a normal person in the presence of a male of my species, he pushes past me, blocking me between the doorway and his ridiculously large body. He smells like sawdust and evergreen.

Nobody has ever offered to stand between me and trouble before. I've never felt so safe or protected. I file the feeling away to investigate again later. When my heart slows and I resume measured breathing and can think straight. Likely not until Brody leaves.

"I'm fine," I answer, closing the door and leaning against it. "There's nothing going on in here. I'm just a dork."

He turns, his gaze taking me in from head to toe. His eyes seem to push into me, pulling out secrets. I can't catch my breath.

Wow. He is just *wow*. So intense, so ruggedly handsome. And burly. He takes up so much room as he dominates the space around him.

"Why do you think you're a dork?" he asks finally.

I shrug. Perhaps he knows nothing about fashion, because one look at my outfit could probably answer that for him. But that's not all. "I don't have a lot of social skills."

He shrugs back. "I don't like people much either."

"It's not that I don't like people. I just don't know how to act around them. I say stupid things." Like now. "It's worse with boys."

"Good thing I'm not a boy then."

That sounds like flirting. Is he flirting with me? I can't be sure. It is the closest I've ever come to flirting though.

Who am I kidding? No guy with biceps that thick would flirt with me. My stupid hormones. I don't know what to do with all these new feelings he's churned up inside me. Because suddenly, I can picture what it would be like to be under him. To have all his attention on me. To be completely filled by him.

Heat pulses between my legs in time with my heart. I am achy and wet and this has never, ever happened to me so strongly before.

The room is so hot. Or maybe it's just me. I'm burning up. I feel needy and want things I don't know how to name.

Maybe after he leaves, I'll visit that porn site again. I've been trying to understand sex. Textbooks only go so far. It's not like I'm getting much help from guys my own age. They're like this whole other alien species to me. I can observe them, make what I think are reasonable deductions about their behavior, but the interacting part never seems to go the way I think it will.

I hear girls talking about sex like it's this great thing, but until Brody knocked on my door, I never felt the sexual attraction they would discuss. Perhaps now that my body has responded this way to an actual person, the porn clips will make more sense. I want to learn how to be aroused and cause arousal in someone else. This will probably require that I spend time outside of class doing things other than studying.

So tonight, after Brody leaves, instead of spending my evening reading the new book I bought about world history, I will try to masturbate while thinking of Brody. My hypothesis is that the way he makes me feel standing here while he is fully clothed will still stimulate me later when I allow myself to imagine him naked. If that is true, then I will once again get wet, and this time when I stimulate my clitoris, I will be able to achieve an orgasm.

It will be my first.

It occurs to me that I am applying the scientific method to making myself come and that perhaps this is why nobody has shown any interest in me as of yet. I am not able to just let go, stop thinking. I don't think it's an attractive trait to young men. Or maybe any men.

Masturbating while thinking of Brody and watching pornographic images is probably as close as this girl will ever get to sexual satisfaction.

CHAPTER TWO

Brody

She is like a nervous bunny rabbit. Little Megan Jennings dresses like she's going to church. She's buttoned up to her neck and covered with a cardigan and sensible shoes. Like maybe she's sixty. At the same time, she has this innocence I don't come across much in the women I meet. It goes beyond her makeup-free face and little clip holding her bangs to the side, the rest gathered into a low ponytail. If I hadn't been told she was going to college, I'd have assumed she was younger. Her glasses take up half her face, but I can still see the cute freckles dotting her cheeks.

Everything about her is packaged to keep a man from looking twice.

But something about that makes me keep looking.

For a moment there, when I thought something was going on in the house and she was scared, I was ready to do whatever needed to be done to make her safe. That's not my standard operating procedure. Maybe it's because she's so small. Maybe it's because I can't really get behind the idea that her old man was fine with me coming over when she's alone, defenseless. Hell, he even told me he was gone for a week. What kind of father tells a man like me, a man he doesn't even know, that his house and daughter are unprotected and for how long?

A stupid one. That's what kind.

I'm not the kind of guy you leave in your house alone. But I'm *really* not the kind of guy you leave unsupervised in your house with your daughter.

He probably thinks, like she obviously does, that her appearance is some kind of deterrent. That it makes her less desirable. Invisible.

But they are both wrong.

Her clothes make me wonder what she looks like under them. Her hair makes me want to take it out of its band and spread it out on my pillow while she's wearing nothing but those damned glasses and I'm pumping her deep. The racing pulse in her throat makes me want to chase her harder—she is prey to me. I am a wolf.

But I'm also a businessman. I'm not going to screw my client's daughter just because I can.

And she's too fucking innocent. I should leave her be.

But I can *think* about fucking the innocence right out of her all I want. And I intend to. Later. After my work is done.

I just can't ever act on it.

She shows me upstairs. We pass her room, and I catch a glance of the pink walls. The pretty lace bedspread. A poster on the wall of the Periodic Table of Elements.

I can't stop the smile on my face. I've never thought the words "cute" and "nerdy" about someone I wanted to fuck before. Nothing about her is my type.

"I won't be too long," I tell her when she directs me to the office down the hall from her sweet bedroom. "Just taking some measurements today. So I'll be out of your hair and you can invite your boyfriend over and take advantage of having the house to yourself this week."

Her blush paints her face instantly. Fuck. I want to see how low that pretty pink goes.

She pushes her glasses up her nose. "I don't have a boyfriend."

I don't know why that relieves me. I can picture exactly what kind of guy she'd date. Some kind of fucking computer genius—the kind that get beat up in high school and end up owning the mansion and a private jet by the time they are thirty. He'd be tall, too skinny, and awkward. But he'd treat her nice and take care of her. And she deserves to have it all.

And I fucking hate this guy I made up.

It's been too long since I got laid if I'm obsessing about this bookworm and her boyfriend, real or not.

It's been two years since I got serious about my business, and I haven't been with anyone since. I got tired of the old crowd. Spending every night at the bar, sleeping with chicks I wouldn't talk to sober, and getting in bar fights over stupid shit just didn't do it for me anymore. Getting arrested for being drunk and disorderly hit the final nail. I wanted something else for myself. A better life than the one my old man has. And that's the direction I saw myself going while I sat in the drunk tank—a one way ticket to Loserville.

My dad drinks like it's his second job only because smoking Marlboros is his first. He hit me until I was big enough to hit back. That's when my ma left him, too. I help her out because she's my mother—but I don't think she trusts that I won't end up like her ex. She doesn't trust anyone.

But I can guaran-fucking-tee I won't hit women or kids like he did. I won't be my old man.

These days, I work, work out, and work on my house. That's about it. My custom woodworking business has taken off in the last year—rich guys like my quality and they appreciate me coming in on time and not fucking up their nice houses. My body appreciates the tension releasing exercise of lifting weights since I stopped getting laid. And my house is the thing I'm most proud of. I built it with my own hands, man. It's not a mansion, but it's mine.

Taking woodshop in middle school gave me an outlet. I've always been good at woodworking. Nobody could have predicted how much I would love it though. It's not a job to me, it's my life.

But judging my reaction to this sweet little nerd, it might be time to do something about my self-imposed celibacy.

"So, Meg, why don't you have a boyfriend?" I ask as she's opening the door to her father's study.

Megan's face falls, and she looks down at her shoes. Shit. I made her feel bad.

A look of determination crosses over her features, and she brings her gaze back up. Not directly into my eyes, but at least it's not down.

But I want her to look into my eyes. I don't know why.

"I'm just not the kind of girl guys go for," she finally says.

Out of nowhere, a surge of primal lust surprises the hell out of me. I want to push her against the wall, yank her skirt up, and show her, balls deep, why she's wrong. I want to fuck her into feeling confident. I don't even remember the name of the last girl I wet my cock on...but I want to use my dick to take care of this girl right here in front of me.

Makes no sense.

"Baby, I don't know who told you that, but you've just been around the wrong guys if you believe it."

Megan shrugs. "I don't have time for dating anyway. With school and practice, I'm too busy."

"You play an instrument?"

She looks down again, shaking her head quickly. She's embarrassed. I'd like to fuck that right out of her, too. She should never be ashamed.

We're in the study now. I should be taking final measurements and getting to work. "What are you practicing?"

"You'll think it's weird."

"Do *you* think it's weird?"

She scrunches her forehead in concentration. The cutest damn thing. "No."

"Then own it, baby. What are you practicing? What keeps you too busy for dating guys who aren't good enough for you anyway?"

She has a dimple. Fuck. I didn't see it before. Maybe because it's the first time I've seen her smile. It fucking undoes me.

"I'm in the *Jeopardy!* contestant pool. My year waiting period was up last month. They'll contact me in the next five months if I make it to the show."

That is...the nerdiest thing I've ever heard. She's like the queen of nerds. And damn if my dick isn't rock hard. I want her bad. I've never wanted a woman more. I feel like I walked into this house and my world flipped or something.

"That's amazing," I tell her. I leave off the part about what I want to do to her body right now. About how I want her to tell me about balancing chemical equations while I pump into her and make her come.

"You don't think that's nerdy?"

It takes me a minute to get back on track with the conversation. I'm too busy trying to adjust my dick without being obvious. What did she just ask me?

Oh, yeah. Nerdy. "No, I definitely think that's nerdy. But that's cool. You shouldn't ever be ashamed of being smart."

That dimple winks at me again. "I'm not ashamed of being smart. It's just...most people...especially guys...they don't think it's all that great. I don't have much in common with very many people."

"Why don't you hang out with other smart people then?"

"I think I'm just too closed off." She pushes her glasses up again. "Though I'm rambling enough to you. Sorry. I'll let you get to work."

She starts to go out, but I put my hand on her shoulder as she passes me. "Don't settle for just anyone." I don't know why I'm telling her this. "There's a guy out there who will be turned on by your brain. You'll find him."

She swallows hard. "I wouldn't know what to do with him if I found him," she says and darts out of the room.

CHAPTER THREE

Megan

Brody comes over every day after my last class. It's a special kind of torture because I love having him around, but it also makes me feel the loneliness even more because now I'm aware of what I can't ever have.

A normal conversation for one thing.

He's always so nice to me, asking me about things I know he has no interest in, but I can't help stammering and getting weird. I've tried watching current television and movies to understand social cues better, but it doesn't seem to do me any good. He's just too big and too masculine and his voice too husky. He short circuits my brain. My reaction to Brody borders on ridiculous. And then there is the rest of my body.

It usually starts with a cold sweat. When I first open the door to him every day, I feel the blood drain from my face and then it fills back in with a hot flush that I know he notices because the corner of his mouth quirks up into a slight grin. Then my heart starts racing like the greyhounds are after me and I'm a rabbit on the track. About then, I find a ball of nervous energy gets lodged in my throat so I can't swallow. I'm sure I'm an attractive picture at that point, but it gets worse. He usually starts a little small talk that I cannot ever hear because the sound of my heartbeat fills my head and I get lightheaded.

That's all well and good, right? I mean, it sounds like a lovely time.

But it gets worse.

Because while I am charming him with all my extremely unattractive nerves, the tingles in my breasts start. They begin to feel achy and full and then, bam! My nipples harden like they're ready to cut glass or something. And the ache travels down, going lower and lower until my panties get moist. And then I want to touch myself. Well, no. I want *him* to touch me. But since that isn't going to happen, I just get achy and needy and wanting. And then he leaves and I spend the rest of the night watching porn and trying to imagine it's not my hands.

I am such a mess.

No man has ever affected me like this before. I'd thought maybe I just had a low sex drive until recently when I started following some sketchy tumblr accounts and then graduated to full-on pornos. It was then I accepted that I had a sex drive—but it wasn't until I met Brody that it revved up for the first time about a flesh and blood person.

And revving isn't great. I wish I could go back to not caring about sex. Not having these messed up feelings.

Not *not* having orgasms. I just can't get there.

I'm always horny and never satisfied. I can get close to coming. But something always slams the door shut before I get all the way through it.

He's upstairs now, doing some sawing or something, and I go to the mailbox. This is also not my favorite part of the day. I want so badly for the letter to come inviting me to be on *Jeopardy!* But that dream also feels too big for me. I'm not good with all these anticipatory feelings. I've always done better with a normal schedule with little variation. Little emotion. Now I anticipate the mail and Brody every day, and feelings course through me that I don't understand.

I used to think I might actually be part android. And I like it better that way. When I don't have all these feels that I don't know what to do with.

I'm sorting through the mail in the kitchen when he pops his head in.

"I need to go check on the custom glass, so I'm leaving early today." He notices the mail in my hands and comes toward me. "Did it come?"

I shake my head. "Not today. Maybe not ever."

"Hey, none of that. Didn't you ever hear about thinking positively?"

I frown. "Thinking positively doesn't change facts. The facts are that they have not invited me on the show and they might not. Even though I passed their requirements and got on the waiting list. It's not logical to assign something intangible like "positive thinking" to a situational problem."

He's smirking at me in that way that he has, but I can hardly be mad at him because the fact that he even cares about whether I get on *Jeopardy!* or not gives me another unfamiliar feeling to deal with. I'm not used to being supported.

I was always the weird kid. My dad never knew what to do with me because I wasn't like other girls my age. I know he loves me, but he doesn't understand me. Which, come to think of it, neither do I. But my dad has tried, over the years, to give me things he thinks I want. Things I would want if I were like his friends' daughters.

But I'm just me. Nerdy. Awkward. Unsure of how to deal with interpersonal relationships. And until recently, mostly asexual.

"Why is it funny to you that I don't think positive thinking is the way to fix a problem."

"It's not funny to me."

"You're smirking at me."

"Okay, it's *amusing* to me," he corrects.

"Why?"

"You live in a world that's so black and white. But the rest of us live in a world with more gray in it. Sometimes, facts don't matter."

"That doesn't make sense."

He moves closer to me. I freeze with my back against the counter as he invades my space. My heart is jackhammering like crazy in my chest. Brody is more wall than man, but I don't feel threatened. The scent of sawdust now tops *bookstore smell* as my favorite scent.

"Some things don't make sense, Megan."

Don't I know it.

He pushes my glasses up on my nose gently. "You can't predict the best things. They just sneak up on you."

"I..." I choke on my words when I notice he's staring at my mouth. My breath hitches and my lips part. "I don't like surprises. Random makes me nervous."

"Life has a funny way of throwing a lot of random at you." He's taken up all the space. All the air. My pussy clenches on itself. I want him. "I'll see you tomorrow. Lock the door behind me." And then he boops my nose.

I can't even believe this is happening to me. It takes forever for my heart to stop racing. For my lungs to regulate my breath.

He booped my nose. Men don't do that to women they want to have sex with. They do that to children. Girls they think are cute and childlike.

I need to get these feelings under control because he doesn't like me the way I like him. Duh. And even if he did, what the heck would I even do with that? He's out of my league.

The only thing I can do is take matters into my own hands. So I go upstairs and begin taking off my clothes.

Maybe this time.

I set up my laptop next to me on the bed and put on the headphones while queueing up my favorite site. Choosing a video to watch, I opt for a teacher/student short, I slip my fingers down to my very wet pussy.

I part my lower lips with one hand and begin strumming with the other. I don't touch my clitoris yet. I want to wait. Draw it out. As I get closer to what I hope is a real climax, I start paying more attention to the bundle of nerves that are begging to be touched. I close my eyes, the aural stimulation from the video enough to get me closer. I wish I had a vibrator. I need to figure out the best way to get one without announcing to my dad that I'm practicing self-love.

I'm close. Really close. I start moaning.

That's when I get the feeling I'm being watched.

My eyes pop open.

Brody.

CHAPTER FOUR

Brody

Fuck. Me. My sweet little nerd is naked except for those glasses. She's spread herself wide, and she's watching porn while playing with that little pussy I only let myself imagine at night when I'm stroking my own dick.

Well, she's not playing with it now. Her mouth is shaped in a surprised "O" and she's blushing. Hell, I'm blushing. I don't think I've ever blushed before.

She sits up quickly, her headphones wire jerking her. "Oh my God!"

I should close my eyes. Turn around. Do something. But I just stare, and my dick presses against my zipper and I can't stop the gruff noise from escaping my throat when she bends over looking for clothes to cover herself.

"I'm sorry, Megan." I have momentarily forgotten how pissed I was a second ago when I charged up the stairs to read her the riot act for not locking the front door behind me like I'd told her to.

She holds a pillow to her chest. I don't like her covering herself. I have to fight the primal urge to pull the pillow away so I can have my fill of looking at her. I don't know what the hell is wrong with me. I'm a bastard for looking and a bigger bastard for wanting more.

"What are you doing here?"

"I thought you heard me. I knocked. I called your name."

"Oh my God. Oh my God."

I lower my voice, trying to calm her freakout. "I left my wallet in the study, so I had to come back for it. You didn't lock the fucking door behind me."

She raises her eyebrows.

Maybe I am out of line, but I don't give a shit. "What if it wasn't me? You left yourself unprotected. Anyone could have come through that door."

My adrenaline starts pumping again. I'm pissed. Angry at her for not being cautious. Angry at her old man for leaving her unguarded. Angry at myself for not making sure it was locked before I left.

"Right now, I wish it was anyone but you."

Her words are a cold spike into my heart. "What? What the fuck is wrong with you? You could have been raped or worse. You need to protect yourself. What if someone wanted to hurt you?"

She closes her eyes. "This is the most embarrassing moment of my life."

I look around the room and don't see anything readily available to clothe her, so I reach back to pull my own shirt off.

When it's over my head, I catch the incredulous look on her face. "What are you doing?"

I toss her my shirt. "Put this on."

She stares at me. Her eyes big and round, her cheeks white like a ghost.

"What? Did you think I was going to hurt you?" I ask. And I'm the one who's hurt. I thought we had a kind of...I wouldn't call it friendship exactly. But I thought she at least trusted me. "Did you think I would force myself on you? Just because you were naked?"

She twirls her hand to get me to turn around. Like I haven't already seen her? Whatever. I turn.

"I was just surprised to see you taking off your shirt. I know you wouldn't hurt me. And I doubly know just seeing me naked wouldn't make you want to ravish me."

I turn back toward her, ready or not. "What are you talking about?" She's got me so tied up in knots—I think I've gone through every emotion I know in the span of five minutes.

Megan shrugs. "I'm not your type. I'm sure, even naked, I'm not your type. Can you go now? Get your wallet. I'll lock the door this time."

"Megan—"

"Please. I'm mortified enough. Please just leave me alone. I know you didn't mean to see me, and I know I'm...not much to look at. But I do have some pride."

I'm in too deep of water here. She's suffering from a case of confidence that I could fix. That I want to fix. But that would be a horrible idea, no matter what my cock is saying. If I tell her how she turns me on, then I could lose this job. And many other jobs after that. She might even have me arrested. It doesn't look good, me half naked in her bedroom uninvited.

If I don't tell her, she might go on thinking she's undesirable or some shit. I don't want to scare her. But I don't like the hurt in her eyes. Not when I know I could fix it.

Either way, tomorrow is going to be awkward as hell, so I might as well just put her mind at ease.

"Baby, you don't even know how much you turned me on." Fuck, just looking at her in my t-shirt is making me crazy. Knowing she's going to smell like me. Knowing my skin has touched where her skin touches. "You're fucking beautiful."

She shakes her head slowly.

I take a step closer to her bed. Slowly. Trying to make sure she doesn't feel trapped or intimidated. But part of me wants her to be a little wary. I'm a fucking predator now. I want her to know it. I want to see it in her eyes. "You are. I don't know who told you that you aren't my type, but they were wrong."

"I'm nobody's type," she tells me in a small voice. "I've never...you know." She realizes that her laptop is still playing porn, so she closes the lid and covers her face. "Oh my God."

"Don't be like that, Meg. Don't be embarrassed." Is she trying to tell me she's a virgin?

She's naked and untouched. My blood is pumping so much to my dick, it's a miracle the seams of my jeans are holding up.

"Don't be embarrassed? You just walked in on me masturbating."

"And I liked it. A lot." I cup my cock through my jeans. "A whole hell of a lot."

Now that the first rush of her embarrassment and my anger has run its course, my mind keeps replaying the vision of her lush body. Her round, small tits. Her flat tummy. The way her hips flare out slightly, hinting at a voluptuous shape.

Her perfect pink pussy. She's not shaved like the women I usually see. The ones I used to bang from the bar or the ones in porn. That makes it even hotter for me. She's perfect the way she is. I don't know why. Maybe that makes me some kind of pervert.

I can tell by her wary expression that she doesn't believe me, but her eyes are drawn to my growing package and she blushes. "I've never been asked out on a date. That's why I know I'm nobody's type. I've never been kissed. Never...you know..."

"Been fucked?"

Her eyes go owl-big under those big black framed lenses. She's not used to rough language. I guess I've tried to keep it polite between us, but when I get turned on, my mouth goes directly to dirty talk and swearing.

Everything about her is calling to my primal instincts now.

"Say it," I tell her. I can't stop myself now. Something feral inside me grows stronger every minute I'm in this pink room. I can smell her, and it jacks me up.

"Say what?"

"That you've never been fucked."

"I'm...I'm a virgin."

I shake my head. Lower my voice even more so she knows I'm serious. That I'm in charge. "Say it," I demand.

I want to dominate all that sweet shyness. Make her submit it to me. Claim her.

She takes a deep breath. "I've never been fucked."

Fuck. I should go. I know I should. But knowing she's never even been kissed is the hottest thing she could have told me. Like an erotic challenge.

I don't back down from challenges. You didn't get far in my neighborhood if you did.

"You've never seen a guy's cock before?"

She glances at the closed laptop.

"I mean a real man's cock, baby. Not a movie."

She shakes her head again. Swallows hard. Fuck. I want her so bad. I've never wanted anyone like this before. I want to fuck her, yeah. But I want to make her feel good. Not just physically. I want to make her feel whole. Take that sadness and shame away. Who the hell am I to think I can do that for her?

But I'm too gone to turn back. "Say it," I tell her again.

"I've never seen a real man's cock."

"Do you want to?"

CHAPTER FIVE

Megan

I wheeze in a breath. *Do I want to*? Do I want to see a real man's cock? Is he offering?

It's better if I just don't say anything. I've embarrassed myself enough for one day.

"Fair is fair," he says. "You might not be so mortified if you see me the way I saw you."

I blink at him. "You're going to masturbate? In front of me?"

"If you want me to I will. Tell me you want me to."

My shy-girl side is freaking out, but my nerdy science brain is calculating the odds of this ever happening again and how it would be good to have some clinical data to refer to in the future.

A real man's cock. Brody's cock in those big hands. I couldn't stand it. "Yes. I want to see you pleasure yourself."

"No. Say you want me to stroke my cock. I want the words, dirty girl."

His words were making me so wet. "I want to see you stroke your...cock. I want to watch." I push my glasses up. "Now, please. If you don't mind."

He gets that grin again, but I don't much mind. I sit up, ready for the show, aware that I can smell him all over me right now because I'm wearing his shirt. This might be as close as I get to sex with a man. I mean, we're in the same room and everything.

It's now that I realize just how good he looks with no shirt. He's muscled like crazy. His shoulders taper to a trim waist. His abs ripple. A line of hair starts below his belly button and travels to the waist band of his jeans. I want to touch it, follow it with my hand, but I won't. I'm too shy.

He reaches down to unlace his work boots, his eyes not leaving mine as he kicks them off. His big hand moves to the button on his jeans. "Breathe, Megan."

I exhale, wondering how long I've been holding my breath.

"Are you sure you want to see it? You know I'd never force you to do anything you don't want."

Brody is a big man. A solid man. And he could physically force me. But I know, somehow, that he would never. That he has a moral code I can count on. I'm probably too trusting, but then again, I've never really trusted anyone else before.

I want to trust him. I need to trust him. And I'm tired of being annoyed with myself. If I'm not ready, I need to make myself ready. I can't always be the awkward girl alone in her room. A bit of calm settles over me, and I force myself out into the strange new world.

"Take out your big cock, Brody. I want to see it. I want to watch you."

He raises his eyebrows. "It's been hard since I saw you, baby."

He takes down his jeans and underwear in one pass. His cock is jutting out. I look at the thick, hard length of him. It's pointing at me. It's skin looks smooth but for one jutting vein that runs the length of his shaft. He strokes himself a couple of times using the moisture at the head for lubrication.

My core clenches, and my own wetness coats my inner thighs.

"Do you like that? Do you like my cock, sweet girl? You made is so hard."

I whimper. "Yes."

"Do you feel less embarrassed now? I've seen yours, you've seen mine. Are we even?"

I shake my head. No. I don't want this to be over yet. This memory might have to last me a lifetime. "I want to watch you come." So much. Is it like the porn? Or is that staged?

Brody groans. "Fuck, Meg." He continues to stroke. Even in his big hands, his cock looks huge. It is getting even harder, thicker. I want to get a ruler and note his measurements in a notebook.

But that would be supremely nerdy and break the mood, so I go back to just watching intently.

"Megan, when I come, it's going to be messy. Are you sure you want me to do it here? In your pretty room?"

Oh, I like this dirty talk. I love the rumble of his voice and the way he makes everything sound so filthy.

I move to the edge of my bed on my knees. "Yes. Please. Show me."

"Help me along then, sweetness."

"How?" I can't believe this is happening to me. Last week, I couldn't get the skinny, freckled boy at Starbucks to engage in small talk. Now I have a giant naked man in my bedroom asking if I'm sure I want him to come. "How can I help you?"

"Keep talking to me. Show me your tits. I'm easy."

"My breasts are small."

"Your tits are perfect."

There isn't much point in pretending to be a prude at this point, so I lift his shirt off of me and bare my breasts for him. "I saw a movie on the computer where he came on her tits."

His body tenses, and he moans and then resumes his stroking. "Do you want me to do that? Do you want me to come on your tits?"

In for a penny, I guess. "Yes. I want you to come all over me."

"Fuck." His pace increases, and he stares at my chest while he steps closer to my bed. "Your tits are perfect." He already said that, but since I don't mind the repeat, I don't tell him.

His cock is an angry purple now. I wonder what it feels like, but I'm not ready to be so bold as to ask to touch him. The sound of him frapping it and the increasing harshness of his breath tells me he is close to orgasm. I remember in the movie, she held up her breasts, so I slide my hands to my own. Cupping them as an offering. A canvas. "Come on me," I whisper.

And he does. He roars and ropes and ropes of it land on me. Painting me with his seed. I'm so turned on, I'm rocking my hips as more come hits me. I had no idea how hot it would be to be covered in a man's come.

He collapses into my desk chair like he's boneless, and I'm oddly satisfied that I had a part in bringing him to this point. He could have any woman he wants. But today, I made him come so hard he can't stand up. And I didn't even touch him.

His breathing slows down, and he lifts his head. "We're not even. I just remembered I didn't get to see you come."

I shrug. "It's okay. I don't think I can."

He lifts his brow and clenches his jaw like I just pissed him off. "What do you mean?"

"I think there might be a biological impairment on my end. I find I am unable to reach a climax."

"If I parse out all those big words, I think you're trying to tell me you don't think you can come."

I push my glasses up. "That is correct."

"Challenge fucking accepted."

CHAPTER SIX

Brody

Megan is the prettiest thing I've ever seen, kneeling on the lace cover, her chest iced with my come.

"You think you can help me achieve orgasm?" she asks.

My dick twitches, already getting primed again. "I can make you come, Megan," I assure her.

I shouldn't be here. I don't belong here. But fuck if I'm leaving without getting this girl off.

She purses her lips and gets that now-familiar wrinkle above her nose. "I realize this might sound strange, as we are both naked in my bedroom, but I have some trepidation about losing my virginity this afternoon."

I love the way she talks. So methodical. So many big words. None of the "ums" and "likes" and "ahs" most girls use.

"We don't have to have sex for you to come. I think I just proved that all over your chest."

She blushes. "I would expect if things go any further, that most men would expect..."

"I'm not most men, baby. This is all about you." I stand up, my cock getting bigger so she knows for sure that it's not that I don't *want* to fuck her, but that I'm not going to. Yet.

Because sometime in the last two minutes, I've decided that this girl is mine. She's what I've been waiting for. What I didn't even know I wanted. It makes sense now why I stopped sleeping around. Why I didn't want anyone else. She's it for me.

Hell, maybe I knew from the first time I saw her. When I thought she might be odd but someone I needed to look out for. When I could see under the prim clothes and overthinking was a girl who wanted my jizz on her chest. Feels like more, though. Feels like something I don't know words for.

"Stay there a minute," I tell her and go into the bathroom. I get a warm washcloth and a towel, and when I get back into her room, I kneel in front of her. "May I?" I ask and bring the warm cloth to her chest to clean her up.

I can see her pulse jumping in her neck. And this close, I can smell her pussy, and it's making my mouth water. It makes me crazy. She makes me crazy. I want her so bad. I want to mark her. Make her mine. Claim her. But I know I have to wait until she's ready. I have to hold back.

But I can make her come. "I'm going to get you off."

My face is very close to hers. It feels intimate just being near without closing eyes. Without kissing. She doesn't pull away, but her eyebrows pull together. "What if I can't?"

"You can. I promise. You need to get out of your head. Turn off that sexy brain of yours for a bit." I breathe her in. Let her settle into my lungs. And then it's time. I grab her laptop and put in on the desk. "You need to give up control of everything to me for a little while. Can you do that, baby?"

"I...I don't know."

I cup her jaw firmly in my hand. "Look at me." When she does, I feel like a king. "I'm in control now. You have to trust me. That's all you have to do. Trust me and listen to me. Give yourself to me completely. That's all."

She nods, and I take her glasses off. "Good girl." I push her gently onto her back. My dick is leaking pre-cum like a faucet she's got me so worked up.

"Spread your legs."

She obeys immediately, showing me her pretty cunt. Fuck. She's soaked. Hell yeah, she's gonna come. "Getting you off is going to be my pleasure, nutmeg."

She sighs and closes her eyes.

"Look at me." She opens them. "Your pussy is mine now. Do you understand?" She nods. "Tell me."

"My pussy belongs to you," she answers without hesitation.

That is the hottest damn thing I ever heard.

"You don't need to worry about coming. Everything is under control. Just relax. I've got this."

I get down between her thighs and breathe her sweetness in. I'm gonna bust a nut just licking her, I know it. So I begin. I nuzzle her lips open with my nose and then snake my tongue into her juicy pussy. I moan with the pleasure from her taste. Where has this girl been? She's made to be mine.

She jerks and makes a keening sound that revs me up even more.

"You smell so fucking good, baby. Do you trust me?"

"I trust you, Brody."

Fuck, yeah. I lap at her juices, holding her legs still as she writhes under my mouth. I'm not even going to have to finger her. She's grinding against my face and crying out already. I'm drinking her in when her whole body tenses. Her hands find my hair and she holds me there against her clit. Flooding me.

"I'm coming," she cries. "Thank you. Thank you. Thank you," she sobs.

But I'm just getting started. I can't get enough of that sweet, innocent pussy. I keep eating her out, leaving her clit alone for a few minutes until she starts getting extra juicy again. My face is covered in her pussy juice, but nothing could pull me away from her. Not a damn thing. I want to devour her.

Her voice is hoarse, and I'm humping her sheets. She comes for the third or fourth time, and I let go of my own load all over her girlish bed. The air is thick with the scent of us. And still I want more.

I want in that pussy. But I'll wait until she's ready.

She's trembling now. Little quakes wracking her entire body, so I move up the bed and spoon her back against my front, holding her close. She fits so good against me. Soft and sweet. I give her a little squeeze. My cock is getting hard again, the fucker, but my girl needs a break. I don't even know what I'm saying to her, nonsense words I guess, as I stroke her shoulders and arms. Her shakes slow down and I realize she's fallen asleep. I hold her a while longer, though, because I can.

I take her pony tail out of the hair band and run my fingers through her long, dark hair. I think about what it would be like if I were winding it around my hand and pulling while I'm balls deep in her heat. I wanna make her say dirty, filthy things. I want her to beg for my cock. But I also want to hold her tight and fuck her slowly until she doesn't know where she ends and I begin. Until we are one.

I don't know what happened to me this afternoon, but my life is different now. I thought I got my shit together the last few years so I wouldn't turn into my old man. But I think I got it together so I could be worthy of this. Of her. She's nothing like anyone I ever met. She's so smart, but she's unprotected out in the world. Nobody looks out for her. Nobody puts her first.

I will.

I may never understand the things she talks about, the things she knows—I barely graduated high school and have no desire to go to college. I'm not stupid, though. I'm not even that bad at *Jeopardy!*

And I understand the important things. She'll never doubt that she's wanted. Cherished. Fuck. I sound like a goddamned romance novel.

It's too soon to make sense. I know that's what people will say. But hell, what do other people have to do with us? She balances me. Makes me want to be a better man. Makes me hope for more than just the financial security I've been working on. She makes me want a life. A real one. Nights with my girl watching stupid shit on TV and laughing. Someone to take care of. To take care of me. Kids someday.

Fuck. Who the hell am I? Yesterday, I didn't think I would ever want a family, not after growing up in my fucked up clan. But now I can see it. Someday. I could be a good dad if I put my mind to it. My wife and kids would never be afraid of me losing my temper. I'd never spend money meant to take care of them on cheap booze and smokes. I could teach them stuff. Stuff my dad never took the time to show me. And they'd be smart like their mom. Maybe my kids would cure cancer or some shit.

I bury my face in her neck, and she sighs in her sleep. I'm getting ahead of myself. Megan will need to go slow. She's too unsure of herself to jump into anything. I'll have to be patient. Earn her trust. Show her that she's perfect the way she is. That I like her dorky side as much as I like her tight little body.

She said she trusts me.

She's going to be mine.

She is already mine.

CHAPTER SEVEN

Megan

I'm pacing the entryway because Brody will be here soon and I have to let him in and I don't understand what we are now. Or how to act. I mean, I didn't understand before, either. But now I doubly don't understand. If that is a thing.

I didn't get much sleep last night after he left. I slept fine while he was there, though. In his arms. Cocooned in his heat and the hard planes of his body. I felt so safe and at peace.

"At peace" is not something a person like me feels very often. Always living in your brain means never really feeling comfortable in your body. And your brain never shuts off. Maybe it was the orgasms, but I suspect it was the orgasms *and* being held by Brody that allowed my brain to rest.

For that short time, I had nothing to worry about. When Brody told me, "I've got this," right before he rocked my world off its foundation, I let go. For the first time maybe. I knew he would care for me. I knew there was nothing to do or think or worry about. I even felt sure that he wanted me. That he desired me. I've never, ever felt that before.

I trusted him.

But now I don't know how I feel.

I don't know if he wants me still or again. I suspect that it was a one-time thing brought on by the extenuating circumstances of my epic and humiliating masturbatory show. But after watching him take matters into his own hands, I understand why it was sexually stimulating for him to see me with my hand in my own pussy. We are just animals underneath it all. Being turned on isn't the same thing as desiring someone.

I spent a lot of time last night reliving the hours he spent in my bedroom. Having an orgasm is the highlight of my college career so far. Having Brody want me like that is the highlight of my *life* so far.

But how does Brody feel today? He knows my nerdy side, and now he knows me naked. Does he want a repeat? Does he expect a repeat? Does he think we should have sex now?

Do I want to have sex now?

I think about his large penis...no...that sounds clinical... I think about his monster cock...and think yes, very much I want to have sex now. But then again, he was big. Too big perhaps. I fear he's not a starter penis.

And he's not a starter boyfriend. Brody's too intense. Too alpha. Even experienced girls would have trouble not drowning in his testosterone. I'm afraid he'll swamp me.

I'm also afraid I'll fall for him. That would be the worst. The hardest. Because he's got broken heart written all over him. And I know I'd never recover. My heart is not as strong as my brain. I have to be sure when I give it to someone. I'm the kind of person who can only give it once. If I don't choose wisely, I'll be damaged forever.

The doorbell rings.

I inhale too deeply, choking on my breath. I'm still coughing a little when I swing the door open.

God, he's beautiful.

Now I know too much. I can't unsee how he looks under his clothes. I understand lust now—how it grabs hold and shakes you like a ragdoll.

My clothes feel uncomfortable and restricting. I want to tear them off. Tear his off as well. This would not be logical as we are standing in front of the door. But logic seems to be failing me.

"Are you going to let me in, little girl?" he drawls the double entendre a little too confidently. Like he's reading my mind. That I'm amusing him again.

I straighten my spine. I don't want to amuse him. I don't want to be a joke to him. I want a level playing field, but I don't know how to get to it. I'm at the bottom of the cliff face and a level field seems a long way up. "I haven't decided yet."

He smiles. A real one. I think my heart just doubled in size. "Oh, you're going to let me in. All the way in. Just a matter of time."

Well, then. That answers one of my questions. He wants me again. Maybe.

God. This stuff is so hard.

I take extra time making sure to swing the deadbolt after I let him in so I can breathe a little longer. When I turn, he's watching me very closely. He takes a step closer, caging my head between his arms and the door. "How are you doing today, sweetheart?"

"I...I'm..."

He's so close. His eyes are burning with a dark fire. "Have you been thinking of me?"

I nod. "Yes."

Then his mouth crashes down onto mine. He swallows my gasp, and I clutch his shirt. We didn't kiss last night. Well, I didn't kiss him. He kissed me plenty, just not my face. But he is mimicking the things he did to me last night, only this time to my mouth. Plunging his tongue inside, tasting me. It's too much and not enough, so my hands creep up his rock-hard chest and loop around the back of his neck so I can bring him closer.

A guttural groan escapes his throat as he grasps my hips while he grinds into me like he can't get close enough. He moves to my neck, sucking and biting. I think he means to leave a mark. I want him to. I want proof when I look in the mirror that this is real. That somehow I made this big man want me this much.

He palms my butt and lifts. "Wrap your legs around my waist."

As soon as I do, he's grinding me harder into the door at my back. The tingle in my pussy grows into a throb.

"Did you make yourself come after I left?"

His cock is so hard, and it's pushing against my clit relentlessly. He asked me something…what was it? "Oh!" I shout as the fireworks start behind my eyelids. He pauses, waiting for me to answer him.

I nod. "Yes. Yes I can do it now. I don't think I'm broken anymore." In fact, I think I'm pretty close to having another orgasm right now.

Maybe I shouldn't have told him. Now he knows he solved my orgasm problem, and maybe he won't help me out with it anymore.

He pushes into me harder. I'm so close to coming again. I'm like a coming machine after yesterday.

"I'm gonna watch you make yourself come sometime," he says, then buries his face in my neck, inhaling deeply. "But this one is mine." He starts using those big hands to manipulate my hips so that I'm rubbing against him again. The tingling sensation starts in my toes and works its way up my body. "Come on me again, nutmeg."

My fingers dig into his shoulders as I shatter from the inside out. But he doesn't relent.

"Fuck, that's so hot. I could watch you come all fucking day."

Well, that's good. Because I'm coming again.

After I stop crying out, he kisses my forehead. He's moved one hand up to cup the back of my neck, the other is still supporting my butt as he pushes us away from the door and carries me to the couch in the living room. He's murmuring things to me, but I'm only getting broken bits here and there because I'm still out in the stratosphere somewhere. I hear things like, "good girl" and "mine now" but it takes a few more minutes for me to realize we're sitting on the couch. He's cradling me in his lap, and he's alternating his words with kisses to my temple.

He's holding me. It shouldn't be such a strange sensation to be held. It's amazing. I burrow into him more, and he laughs.

"That wasn't supposed to happen," he says after a few more minutes of silence.

I freeze up. He didn't want it to happen. He hadn't meant for...wow am I ever lame. I stiffen as much as I can, already missing the smell of his skin. But I need to pull away.

He holds me tighter. "Relax. That's not what I meant. Come back here." He pushes my head back down, my nose back into his neck.

"What did you mean then?" Because I might be about to cry and I've not had much experience with that either.

"I wanted to ask you out on a real date. Treat you right. But then I looked at you, and all I could think of was making you come. It's addictive. You're like my drug, nutmeg."

I relax. And then tense up. Wait, what? "You want to take me out on a date?"

"Yeah. For starters."

Starters?

"I've never been on a date."

"I'm going to take care of a lot of your firsts."

His words fill me with a momentary sense of peace, but then my mind is whirring with all the things I might need to do to get ready for a date. All of my clothes are wrong. My hair is boring. I don't know how to wear makeup. And God only knows what would happen if I tried to wear the only pair of heels in my closet out of the house. So far, they've been a "walk around the bedroom to practice" piece of my wardrobe.

"Relax. I can see the smoke coming out of your ears from all your thinking. It's just a date. It's just us."

"That doesn't help, Brody. People are going to look at you and wonder what you are doing with me. You don't have to take me out in public. I'm not sure I'm ready for that. I don't expect—"

He puts a finger on my mouth to stop my verbal diarrhea. "You should start expecting." He takes his hand back, and I take a quick breath to start talking again, so he puts it back on my mouth. "For one thing, you care too much about what people think. If they pay any attention at all, they'll see two people trying to have a normal dinner together. They might notice you are nervous. They might also see that I'm possessive as fuck about you and stay out of our way."

He pulls his hand away again, but gives me a look that says he's not above shutting me up again if I start doubting him. "Why would they see that?"

"Because I am."

"Why?"

"Why is the sky blue? Things just are. I want to take you out because I want you to see that you deserve to be taken out. But I also want to take you out because I want some good lasagna and good company."

"I actually make a good lasagna," I tell him. Ignoring the part about the good company.

"You cook?" he asks.

"Quite well. Would you like me to make you a meal here?" *Please*?

"Next time. Tonight, I'm taking you out. And...if you're down with it... back to my house."

"Why?"

"My bed is bigger."

Oh. *Oh.* "Um."

"We don't have to fuck tonight. But I want to have you in my bed. I want my sheets to smell like you."

He doesn't have to do any of this. I think of all the data I've accumulated over the years about why I'm undesirable and why a hot guy like Brody doesn't have to put any work into getting a woman in his bed, but especially one like me, and none of it correlates with what he is telling me. That he wants to wine and dine me. That he wants to cuddle for God's sake.

"You don't have to go through all this. You could have had me against the door," I say. My heart is balancing on a tightrope. This could go so very badly. I want to trust that this is real. I want to feel the way I did last night when he told me he'd take care of everything if I just gave him my trust.

"Baby, I could have had your cherry last night. We both know it. And I want it. And I'll get it. But I want more than that sweet little pussy, no matter how tempting it is. I want this," he tapped my head, "and I want this," he put a hand over my heart. "And before you ask, I don't know why. Maybe on paper, we're not a good fit. But the minute I saw you, I wanted to protect you, make you mine. I like it when you tell me the stuff going on in your brain. I like it when I can make that dimple pop out. I like it when your eyes go soft and you come calling out my name. I figure there's plenty more about you that I'm going to like learning about."

This couldn't possibly be my life right now.

"You're doubting me again," he says. "Maybe it will take you some time to gather all your scientific evidence and come to a conclusion about me. I'm not worried."

"What's it like to have all that confidence?" I ask.

"I'm not arrogant. I mean, I have confidence in my work. But the reason I know it's right between us is all on you."

Well, that can't be possible. "Me?"

"You don't trust easy. I get that. Neither do I. But you told me about your dreams when we first met. You let a big guy who intimidated you right into your house. You trusted me last night to help you. And you were never afraid of me. Because deep inside, you know that I'm good for you. And you're good for me." He picks up my hand and kisses it. "It's your trust in me that gave me the confidence to ask you out."

My heart starts racing. "Seriously, we can just stay here." Because the things he is saying, the way he is looking at me, makes me want to take him upstairs right now.

I'm so afraid I'll screw this up.

"Nope." He sighs heavily. "I have work to do in the study now. Be ready at six."

He rolls up and puts me on my feet.

"Brody, I don't know how to dress for a date. I'm not good at the girl stuff. I don't want to embarrass you."

"Wear what you're wearing now." He leans over and whispers into my ear, "Maybe skip the panties."

CHAPTER EIGHT

Brody

Fuck me. My heart stalls as I take her in.

My little nerd may not think she knows "girl stuff," but when she comes down those stairs for our date, I need to pick my tongue up off the floor.

She's hot as fuck.

But my girl isn't wearing a tight mini-skirt with stilettos. She didn't paint her face with layers of makeup. And she's not wearing the kind of perfume that enters the room before the woman does.

Doesn't matter. She's my kind of hot.

I told her we'd go to a nice neighborhood place. Someplace with good food, but where it wasn't too fancy. Just normal people eating dinner and relaxing. She didn't need to dress up, which made her shoulders lose their tension.

I heard her showering a while ago. And it damn near killed me not to join her. Knowing she was in there, naked and soapy, was a special kind of torture.

And maybe she wasn't ready at exactly six, but that is okay too.

She's worth the wait.

She's wearing one of those cardigans she likes so much, but it's a little smaller than usual, and she's not wearing anything underneath it. Its buttons start pretty low, exposing a whole lot of skin and cleavage. Her skirt is longer than most chicks her age wear, but it's hella tight. If she is wearing panties, they're definitely G-string. But that dimple is out on her cheek, and I'm thinking she took my advice and left the panties in their drawer tonight.

She left her hair down and loose, her bangs pulled to the side with one of those clips she likes so well. And those fucking glasses, man. When did I get so hot for glasses?

My cock is stirring, and her gaze drops down to it like it called her. She blushes and looks away. *It's all for you, baby.*

I know I told her we could go slow. But my cock feels like a lead pipe in my pants, and we haven't even started the date.

We get to Rizoli's, my favorite pasta joint, and she's sitting ramrod straight in her chair. "Megan, relax."

She fidgets. "I don't know what to do with my hands."

So I take them into mine. They're tiny. Like she is. But I wanna see them on my cock. Bad.

"Why are you being so nice to me?" she asks.

"I like you. Why wouldn't I be nice to you?" She's on the losing edge of a doubt war, so I have to turn it around fast. "Tell me everything you know about the equator."

She scrunches her face up. "What? Why?"

"I'm interested."

She's still pondering that when our food arrives, but when the waiter leaves, she tells me, "It would take just under a year to walk the equator at three miles per hour."

She knows something about everything, and after an hour of trivia, penne, the best bread in the United States, and a cheesecake that made me jealous the way it got her moaning, Megan is finally relaxed. My dick is not. But I take a lot of pride in knowing I can loosen that tension in her shoulders.

While we wait for the check, I palm her knee beneath the table, causing her to gasp. "Do you still want to come to my place?"

I press my thumb into her flesh lightly and watch her chest rise and fall more rapidly. Those perfect breasts just taunting me.

"Yes," she says finally.

"Are you wearing panties under that skirt?"

She blushes her answer. She's not.

"Are you wet?"

She nods slowly.

"Are you thinking about me? Is that why you're wet? Are you remembering how I made you come?"

"Yes," she whispers.

"You're a very good girl, Megan."

I have a hard time figuring the tip, knowing she's bare.

"When we get in the car, I want that skirt bunched around your waist and your legs open. I'm going to finger you the whole way home."

And I do. I only take my hand out of her pussy to lick my fingers.

When we get to my place, I'm suddenly the nervous one. My cabin is on the outskirts of town. It's small, but it's something I built with my own hands. I want her to like it. I want her to want to be here with me. I've never brought a woman here—or to any place I've lived before.

"You made this?" she asks again on her second tour of the floor plan.

"Yeah." *Do you like it?*

"I'm really impressed, Brody. It's beautiful." She looks around the room. "And it suits you."

My muscles loosen, and I release my breath. She likes it. "How does it suit me?"

"It's rugged but comfortable."

"Is that how you see me?" I'm in her space now. And she has that cute little hitch in her breath when she realizes what I've got on my mind. I slide my hand down her back, pull her in closer. She swallows hard, but her eyes are dilated, and her nipples are poking proudly against that tight sweater. Yeah, she wants me. She's primed for me, and that gets me so fucking hot.

"I'm going to kiss you now," I tell her.

She whimpers and nods.

"That's not how this works, baby."

"I want you to kiss me," she says, her voice a little stronger.

"Where?" I tease, placing a small one above the top button of her sweater.

"Everywhere," she moans. "But start with my mouth. Please, Brody. Kiss me breathless like you did this afternoon."

I take her mouth, slipping my tongue inside her sweetness, and she practically purrs. She stretches up on tiptoe to reach me, and everywhere her body touches mine is like electrical currents zapping lines straight to my cock.

I don't want to scare her, but it feels like there is a feral beast inside me, and I'm real close to losing control. I don't think I'm going to be able to be as slow and patient as I'd wanted to be.

"I'm going to kiss every goddamned inch of your body tonight, baby." I wrap her hair around my hand and pull it until she exposes the arch of her throat to me. I lick her neck, tasting her nervousness. "You're going to get every inch of me tonight. Are you ready for that?" I slide my hand under her sweater and cup one of her tits over the straining nipple. "If you say yes, there's no going back. I'll make it good for you. I'll make you come on my dick until you pass out from pleasure, but I'll own you. I'll never let you go. Is that what you want? Be sure. Because once I take your virgin pussy, it's you and me from here on out."

And I fucking mean it. If she says no, I'll probably die, but I'll take her home. But she takes me inside her tonight, and she's mine. Forever.

I'm still playing with that nipple, waiting for her to commit to me. To us. "I can't think when you do that," she says.

"Don't think. Feel."

She clutches my forearms, her chest rising and falling rapidly. "If you own me after you take me, does that mean I own you, too?"

"You already own me, Megan. It doesn't matter if you say yes or not. I'm yours." She'll kill me or save me tonight. Whatever she says next decides my fate. "I'm already fucking yours."

"You're mine?"

I don't have the words she needs. I could show her with my body if she let me. I'll worship her, and she wouldn't ever doubt me again. But I'm not the kind of guy who has all the right words.

"And you decided this after one slightly awkward date where I babbled on way too long about Woodrow Wilson and the Magna Carta?"

"I decided the minute you opened the door to me the first day. But I was sure when you told me you trusted me last night. It was like everything just clicked."

And something just clicked for her. I can see it. She's different. She's still got color in her cheeks, but it's not a blush. She's excited. She's hot for me.

She begins unbuttoning her sweater. "I want you to be mine more than I want anything. Even *Jeopardy!*"

I don't know how I can be so turned on that my dick is gonna have zipper teeth imprinted on it, but I can still laugh. I've never laughed during sex before. But I laugh now. "You can have both of us."

She's shrugged her sweater off her body and onto the floor. "Well, you're a sure thing. *Jeopardy!* maybe not." She looks down at her chest. "Sorry about the bra. It's very...white. And boring."

I trace the strap from her shoulder to the cup. "I don't fucking care about your bra. I just want it on my floor."

"I need..."

"What do you need, baby? You can have anything you want."

"I need you to take control. Like you did last night. I need you to help me stop thinking so hard so I can just feel. I want you to take me out of my head again."

"You want me to dominate you?"

"Completely."

I know exactly what she needs. And I'll give it to her. She'll always have what she needs from me.

I reach down and pull the bottom of her skirt up, baring that pussy to me. "You want me to claim you?" I ask as I dip my finger in her pretty pink folds. "Are you gonna take my cock as many times as I want to give it to you tonight?"

She gives a sweet little whimper. "Yes."

That was the right answer. "I'm going to fill your little body up tonight." I spread her pussy and rub that damp clit. "My fingers, my tongue, my cock." I slide one finger in her hole. Jesus, she's so tight. "When tomorrow comes, you'll know who you belong to." I bring my hand back out, smell it, lick her off my finger. "Mmmm. Baby, you taste so good. Maybe I'll eat you for hours first."

I find the zipper of her skirt and get the damn thing off her while she kicks her shoes away. I pick her up, bride style, and take her to bed.

If I have anything to say about it, she'll never sleep in another.

CHAPTER NINE

Megan

He lays me on the middle of the bed and then switches on a small lamp. "Spread your legs. Show me that sweet little cunt," he says.

I don't know why that turns me on so much. It's just words. It's not logical. But I like it. I like it a lot. So much that I bend my knees and spread my legs wide and let him look his fill. I want him to tell me what to do.

I've always been a good girl. A smart girl. And a feminist. Maybe I shouldn't like it, the way he talks.

But I do.

Lying in his massive bed that smells like him, I want to feel like his plaything. His fuck toy. I want him to make me do things. I need him to.

Maybe it's because he makes me feel so safe, so protected, so free. I trust him. I can just let go. He's got everything under control. I can't mess up. I can't be awkward. I just need to listen to him.

He strips while he stares at my pussy. "You're going to give me that virgin pussy tonight. Show me how you touched yourself."

Well, okay, I'm still a little shy. I feel the heat climb my cheeks.

"I don't mind if you blush, baby. It's just making me harder." He growls a little. "Just do what I tell you."

I bring my hand down. I'm sopping wet. It's almost embarrassing, but he's into it, so I start touching my clit, my hips bouncing off the mattress already.

"That's it. Show me what's mine. Such a pretty pussy. You better stop or you're gonna come all over yourself, aren't you?"

I can only nod, stilling my hand.

"Such a dirty girl. But tonight you only come for me. On my hand. My tongue. My cock."

I moan. His cock is currently all I can see. It's massive. I think it's even bigger than it was last night.

He gets on the bed and pulls my legs wider. "You look amazing all spread out on my bed." He squeezes my breasts, pushing them together and pulling them apart. "You're the only woman I've ever brought here, baby. You belong in this bed. In this house. You understand?"

Only me.

He pinches my nipple, and I arch nearly off the bed.

Every synapse in my brain is overloaded. All I know is sensation. What I feel. What I need. He leans back and strokes his cock. Once. Twice. Then he brings it to my virgin entrance and dips the head of it in my juices, running it up and down my slit. It makes me shiver in delight. "You better tell me what you want."

"I want to touch you. Your cock," I say. I'm not even embarrassed anymore. I'll say whatever word he wants. I'll do any depraved thing he wants.

"Not yet, baby. Later you can touch it all you want, but I don't want to come too soon. I want this in you."

I raise up on my elbows and watch him sliding his big cock around my pussy. "It's so big. Are you sure...?"

"It'll fit. It'll be tight, but it'll fit. I'm going to put all of it in you. You'll feel me everywhere. You'll definitely feel me tomorrow. Every time you sit down." He's oddly proud of this.

Brody pulls his cock away, and I cry out.

"Just a second, greedy girl. I need to taste you." A long lick from him sends me into an unexpected orgasm. I cry out, clutching the bedding beneath me. He keeps his mouth on me as I sky back down. Not licking or sucking, just there. On my pussy. When my shivers slow, he tells me, "You're so perfect, Megan. I don't know how you got to me untouched. But I'm never giving you up."

Brody crawls back up the bed, kissing my body, stopping on my breasts. He growls, and the low, gravelly sound causes my pussy to clench. He sucks each nipple hard, alternating between them. I'm strung like a bow; my toes are clenching to the pull of his mouth. I think maybe I might be dying.

"I need you, Brody. Inside me. Please."

"Whatever you want, baby."

He presses the head of his cock to my opening, slipping just the tip inside. I like the weight of him on top of me. The way he surrounds me. He kisses me, long and hard, and I can't stop moving my hips, trying to draw him in. "There's condoms in the drawer, but I don't want anything between us when I pop your cherry. Do you trust me? I haven't been with anyone in two years. I can pull out."

"I'm on the pill." I don't need to say I'm clean. We both know it. "You can come inside me." His eyes narrow as they bore into me. "If you want to."

"Fuck, Megan. That's the hottest fucking thing I've ever heard." On an anguished groan, he plunges in hard, breaking the barrier between us. He stills as I gasp on a sharp pain-filled breath. And then he holds me closer. "Breathe, baby. Just relax. It will get better. I promise. I will always make it good for you."

I take a few deep breaths, and the pain eases but the fullness does not. I'm not a virgin anymore. I'm a woman. I'm his woman.

He cups my face, forcing my unfocused gaze to his. I think he sees right into me, through me. I didn't know it was possible to feel so close to a person. So entwined. Not just our bodies. Our minds. Our souls.

I can't support the way I feel with any logic. No books could ever explain this peace. This sense of rightness. My whole life, I've felt out of step with the world.

But I'm right where I need to be. Where I belong. I don't know what made him want me or even look twice at me. I don't know how he saw me when everyone else saw through me. Past me.

He takes my mouth viciously. "You're mine now. I'm never letting you go." He gently starts making shallow thrusts, rocking into me. His hand slides down, and he puts pressure on my clit. "Your pussy is so hot, so tight baby. It's like you're squeezing me. Fuck, I want to come right now."

He buries his face in my neck, and I cling to him as each stroke goes faster, deeper. I need more. I'm suddenly restless. A primitive instinct brings my legs up higher around his waist, my feet digging into his ass, my nails scoring his shoulders. "Fuck me harder," I demand.

The room fills with the sounds of us. Our groans and harsh breaths, our bodies slapping, the headboard banging against the wall. My pussy starts clenching, tightening. My skin is too tight. I can't...I can't...the orgasm hits me like the first deep breath after being underwater. I shatter into a million pieces of light.

"Fuck yeah. Beautiful when you come." I hear.

But my peaks and valleys don't stop. I just keep climbing. "Brody."

"Give me another one, baby. And then I'm going to pump you full of my come."

His words send me over again, and he cries out a curse or a prayer and surges into me. Filling me wherever I'm empty.

CHAPTER TEN

Brody

We've been in my bed for thirty-two hours. Sometimes we get out to eat, but most of the time, I feed her in bed. I like the way she looks wrapped in my sheets. I like the way she looks when I rip the sheet off her.

I'm insatiable for her. The way she smells. The way she tastes.

All day, I barely finish spurting when my cock is already getting hard again. I don't know what I'm going to do when the weekend is over and she goes back home.

Already I know she is worried about her homework. I know I need to take her home. She's probably sore. Hell, I'm sore. My dick isn't used to all the action. It's not complaining.

I think about the condoms I put in the drawer next to the bed. The box is still unopened. I just keep filling her body up with my seed. Fuck, that's the hottest. I have never gone raw before. Not once. I didn't know how good it would be.

Still, my girl has plans. Being on the pill isn't a guarantee that I won't knock her up. I have a primal desire, need, to put my baby in her. But I know that's not best for her yet. She wants to finish school, and I want whatever she wants.

But I can't lie. The idea of her round with my baby makes me want to roar like a caveman. And now I'm hard again.

She's snoring softly, all burrowed into me. That's new for both of us, too. We'd never slept with another person in the bed before. I wasn't sure I could, but fuck if I don't have the sweetest dreams spooned against my little nerd. And when I wake up hard, I can just slide right into heaven.

Her phone rings, so I pull it off my charger and roll her onto her back before I kiss her shoulder. "You got a phone call, nutmeg."

She groans and thrusts her hand out for it, not opening her eyes. She swipes blindly, so I hold her still and help her out. The screen says *Dad*.

Fuck.

Megan

"HELLO?"

"Megan, where are you?"

I sit up. "Dad?" It's Sunday morning. I think. He's supposed to fly home tomorrow night.

"I came home early. I was worried when I didn't find you here."

Because we both know I don't usually go anywhere but school.

"I'm at a friend's house." I don't say "studying" or bother making up a lie. He'll be pleased to know I have a friend.

"That's terrific, sweetheart."

See?

"I grabbed yesterday's mail. Megan, there's an envelope from *Jeopardy*!

Everything in me goes fuzzy and still. I clutch Brody's arm. "What does it say?"

Brody's expression is concerned, so I angle the phone so we can both hear.

"I didn't open it, Megan." He pauses. "Do you want me to?"

"No. Yes. No. I don't know."

"Megan, you've been waiting a long time for their answer. Don't you want to read it for yourself?"

My dad sounds concerned. It's...nice. "I didn't think you cared about the show."

"I don't. But you do. I know we're not always very close, but I want you to be happy. You know that don't you?"

I'm obviously still dreaming. A week ago, we said awkward goodbyes with no hug, I couldn't stammer through a conversation with a bagger at the grocery store, couldn't have an orgasm to save my life, and had no real hope of achieving my goal of meeting Alex Trebek.

Now my father is supporting my dream, I have the finest human male specimen on the planet holding my hand, and as smart as I am, I don't know if I can count high enough to tally the orgasms I've had in one day.

And the dream of getting on *Jeopardy!* is close.

Logically, I know they would not send me a letter to tell me *no*. I understand the process well enough to know that if my waiting period runs out, I just try again from the beginning. But, I didn't wake up in a fairytale, so I hold back the anticipation.

And then I look at Brody.

I *did* wake up in a fairytale, actually.

"I'll come home and read it." And then I squeeze Brody's hand. "Dad, will you be there for lunch? I'll make us something. You can tell me about your trip."

"I was planning on going to the office, but…" I hear him breathing. "I'd like to catch up with you also."

I let out the breath I had been holding. "Dad," I look at Brody who's silently encouraging me to take that step with my father. "I'd like to introduce you to someone."

Maybe it's too soon. I know Brody wants me. But he might not be ready to meet my dad. Well, I guess they already met. But not like this.

"Of course," my father says, though his voice is tighter. "Bring your friend to lunch."

CHAPTER ELEVEN

Brody

I'm shocked. I figured she'd have scrambled out of my bed the minute she heard she had mail, but she's just ended the call with her dad, and she's looking at me like she thinks she made a mistake.

"You don't have to come with me if you don't want to," she says, those big, brown eyes wary and reminding me of the day we met.

"I think you know how I feel about coming with you," I say, trying to put her at ease. "But if we do that, then we'll be late for lunch."

I'm joking with her, but I'm feeling like I might throw up. I've never met anyone's dad before. If he's any kind of father, he's going to fucking kill me for what I've done to his daughter. What I'm going to keep doing to his daughter.

What I'm going to do to his daughter right fucking now.

I flip her over and go right to that warm pussy. I got no problem admitting I'm fucking addicted.

We get back to her house an hour and a half later, and he greets me warily, but he's about the same with Megan actually. I get that they aren't close, but it feels like there is this huge gulley between them. When they were on the phone, she seemed surprised that he was even interested in her game show ambition.

They act like polite roommates or something. He obviously never neglected her—but I don't think he ever cherished her. My girl deserves to be worshipped.

She's so fucking smart it's scary. But she's fragile inside. I don't think he knows that.

51

"So," her father says, sizing me up. "You're my daughter's *friend*? I thought you were my carpenter?"

"Dad..."

"I can be both, sir." To Megan, I say, "Your letter, babe?"

She shakes her head. "After lunch. I need to go make it. I want to try a new recipe."

She practically runs out of the room, leaving me there with her old man.

"She's scared," I tell him.

"You think you need to tell me how my daughter feels?" he asks, offended.

I don't answer him. I don't have to.

He's not a big man. I stand over him, and I'm twice as wide. But he's powerful in his own way. He's got authority and money. He's made sure Megan never went without in that way. So I respect him for that.

But, no, he doesn't know how his daughter feels.

He goes to the stand that is set up with booze. Offers me a drink with his hand, which I decline. As he pours himself something in a fancy glass, he tells me, "Your career is over, young man. I don't know what game you're playing with my little girl, but it ends today. Now. And you can make damn sure any future clients you might have had are gone." He holds up his glass like he's reading answers in the bourbon. "She's barely legal. You should be ashamed. I should press charges."

I get that he's pissed. I'd be pissed, too. "She's nineteen. She's an adult. Nobody forced her to do something she didn't want to do. It's her idea that I'm even here today."

Mr. Jennings shakes his head. "You took advantage of her. She's young and impressionable. She's not like other girls her age. She's naïve. Special."

"No offense, but do you even know her?"

He raises his eyebrows in my direction, surprised maybe that I'm not racing around to win his approval? Or at least his forgiveness? "She's lonely."

"Yeah, why is that, Mr. Jennings?"

He downs his drink. "You don't understand. I try. We just...I've never known what to do with that girl. She's always been smart. Even as a baby. Her mom died when she was so little...she was our buffer. When she was gone, I didn't know how to give Megan what she needed. She didn't like being social. Neither one of us has ever known what to do with the other." He looks me right in the eye. "But I love my daughter. I don't see this, whatever it is, working between the two of you for very long. I'll be here when you're gone."

If he was anyone else, I'd break his nose. But he's her father. And since I'm not going anywhere, I need to not make it worse. "I love your daughter, too."

I should have told Megan first. I was afraid it would scare her off, but she deserves to be told first.

"You just met."

"Doesn't matter. She's mine. And right now, she's scared to open that letter. So either I go in there alone or we go together and help her through this."

He looks shocked. "I don't think she wants me." He takes my measure a long time. "You go on."

"You're wrong about that. I think she needs you but doesn't understand how to ask for your help."

He shakes his head. "It's a game show. She could be a doctor or a lawyer. Anything. Why is it so important to her to be on a game show?"

I was surprised too, at first. But she's good. She practiced with me in bed last night, me reading her answers from a website and her telling me the question that goes with it. I've seen the show—who hasn't—but I never gave much thought to the contestants. I never thought I'd know someone who could make it.

"She told me the first time she remembered seeing the show, she was sitting on her mom's lap," I tell him. "That's the only thing she's said about her mom to me."

Mr. Jennings sets down his glass and hangs his head. "That might be the only memory she has of her. My God, all this time it's been about her mother." He laughs, but doesn't seem happy. "My wife didn't even like that show. I only remember her watching it with Megan's grandmother when she was visiting us. They both died in a car accident soon after. Megan was only four." He pours another shot. "I was lost without my wife for a long time. I did my best. I don't think I did very well."

I'm sure he wishes things were different, but I don't have time for his regret right now. "I'm going to the kitchen now. Join me or don't." I'm not worried about what he thinks he can or can't do to my career. He's more bark than bite and it seems to me he's more relieved I'm here than his is angry.

He's got to know the reason she's lonely is him. That a guy like me could walk into her life and sweep her up because her daddy didn't teach her who to watch out for.

That's on him, though. It's too late now. Megan needs me, and I won't let her down. If she wants to go on a fucking game show then game on.

CHAPTER TWELVE

Megan

I put off opening the letter until after lunch, despite my dad and my...boyfriend?...trying to get me to all through the uncomfortable meal.

I can't believe I have a boyfriend.

We're finishing lunch now. While Brody and I are not great conversationalists and the situation is fraught with awkwardness, my dad is excellent at small talk and carries the heavy lifting of discussion despite the unease I sense between him and Brody and the day drinking my father started after I got home.

It's all so strange. Dad and I don't eat together that often, though he says he enjoys my cooking. And now I have a guest, which also doesn't happen...ever. He probably never thought I'd bring a boy home for a meal. I'm sure he gave that idea up several years ago.

Brody is watching me like he thinks I'm going to crack into a million pieces, but I'm not going to. Either I get on the show or I don't.

I'd almost rather not know.

It's clear that not opening the envelope isn't an option, however, so Brody gets out of his chair and kneels on the floor next to my me, a reassuring hand on my knee. I shoot a quick glance at my dad, whose eyes are narrowed, but he doesn't say anything else.

My hands are shaking. I hate this. All this feeling. I'm not sure why I set myself up for it. What if it says *no*? What if the man next to me changes his mind about me? What if my dad loses interest in me again?

"Babe," Brody says, squeezing my knee. "There's smoke coming out of your ears again. Stop thinking so hard and open the envelope. We'll deal with whatever it says."

I nod. Open it. Scan it while holding my breath. Read it again.

"I'm in," I say. "I tape this summer."

I'm swooped into Brody's arms, surrounded by the scent of trees and man. "I'm so proud of you, nutmeg."

My dad is reading it, smiling. "You weren't this excited when I bought you a car."

I wipe the unfamiliar tears from my cheeks. "I appreciate the car, Dad. I appreciate everything you do for me. I know I'm not the daughter you probably expected—"

"Your mom would be so proud. She'd get a kick out of this. And your grandma, wow, she'd just be jealous. She loved that Alex Trebek."

"She did?"

He nods. "Let me get the Champagne. And then after we toast, I want to look at my new office again."

Brody hasn't let go of me. He and my father share some kind of conversation without words. Since conversations *with* words are confusing enough for me, I don't try to decode it.

Brody clears his throat. "I still have another week's work, sir."

"I know. But what you've done looks great so far. Cunningham is going to be livid that mine is better than his."

"Well, you paid me a lot more than Mr. Cunningham did."

The room seems less tense as they look at each other with a little nod of respect.

"I have so much practice to do," I say. One glass of Champagne, then I need to get to work.

When my dad leaves the room. Brody thrusts his hand up my shirt. "You can practice, but you're doing it at my house."

"Brody—"

"Pack a bag, Megan." He squeezes my breast once. Then another time before sliding his hand out of my shirt. "We face everything together now. That's the deal."

"My dad..."

"Your dad knows we're together. I told you last night that once my cock got into you, you were mine. No turning back."

I don't want to go back. "You're so bossy."

"You like it."

EPILOGUE

Megan

Six months later

"Fuck, I can't even. You've never looked hotter."

I look down at my outfit and am sure that is not true. Though I'm nerdy-chic on my best day, I've opted for pinnacle-nerd for the show's taping in order to play a psychological game with my opponents.

We're in the green room awaiting the final preparation. It's my third contest. I'm enjoying myself, and I'm glad to cross this goal off my bucket list, but I miss home. I miss my dog.

Brody and I rescued a puppy a few months ago. The three of us live together in the cabin he built. He lets me cook for him two nights a week. He cooks two nights. We go out twice (I can't break him of Rizoli's at least once a week.) And on Sundays, we have dinner at my dad's.

The plan is for me to finish college and go to grad school. My dad insists on paying for it, though I'm not sure what I want to do with my degrees. I like going to school because I like learning. But I've found I enjoy writing and hope to make that my career someday. There are fewer people to deal with, and most of them can be contacted by email.

"Last one," Brody says, referring to our practice questions. "Ready? Answer is: *Of course, yes.*"

I wrinkle my forehead in confusion. "What?"

Since the topic was U.S. Presidents, I have no idea what he's talking about.

He opens a box, and a sparkly ring flashes at me.

"Brody?"

"That not it. Try again."

My heart pounds wildly. Logic and feelings war inside me. Logically, I know what this means. We've discussed the possibility now and then. But it was a far off future date.

My emotions start unraveling the rest. I know he loves me. I love him. I didn't used to understand what that meant. I used to worry I was even capable of it.

I don't worry anymore. "If the answer is 'of course, yes' then the question must be...will you marry me?"

Everything stops. Time. Thought. Everything. Bringing my gaze down, it lands on his hands. They are massive. They look so strong. Like he could crush things with them, but I know he uses them to create things. Beautiful things. And he uses them to make love to me every night. And he uses them to make me feel when I would rather hide from emotions and the world.

A knock on the door brings me out of my silent reverie. "Five minutes, Ms. Jennings."

"You're gonna take my last name."

I swallow hard. "I haven't said yes, yet."

He knows I'm teasing. "You'll say yes. You like my dick too much to say no."

"Well, that is true. I do like your dick quite a bit."

"Ms. Jennings?"

I have to go. Crap. "I'll be right out!" I call.

Brody gets on his knee. "So, will you take me and my dick forever or what?"

Oh my gosh. He's going to make me cry. I hate crying, and I have to go on TV. "Yes, yes I'll marry you. I love you."

He slams the ring on my finger, slaps my ass, and tells me, "Good luck. Knock 'em dead out there."

We kiss quickly, and I pause at the door before I go to the soundstage. "Brody?"

"Yeah, babe?"

"Do I look okay?" Which is what I asked him five minutes ago that started this whole conversation.

"Never hotter," he repeats.

"Brody?"

"Yeah, babe?"

"I skipped the panties."

He taps his heart, and I know I own it.

Bonus Epilogue

Brody

She doesn't know what she does to me.

My new wife is sitting in the middle of the bed in her wedding dress. Surrounding her is a mountain of books. Because, yeah, my wife is the kind of girl who brings books to her honeymoon suite.

It's fine by me. I like to see her happy.

She's done with school for the semester, but she's cramming fertility books like there's a test coming up. She won't notice I'm watching her for a while. Once her nose is in a book, it takes an excessive force of energy to get her back out of it.

I've got the energy, though. I'm a groom, and it's my wedding night. I'm hornier than I've ever been, and I've been plenty horny. Especially since I met the hot little nerd on my bed.

I'm going to fuck her while she's wearing that wedding dress. That sounds dirty and fucking hot. Megan would use one of her big words—debauch or some shit. I'll say violating an innocent bride in a gown meant to make her look pure turns me on. But everything my wife wears turns me on.

I'm still wearing most of my tux. We had a formal wedding for her dad's pleasure, and a very short reception for ours. But not as much pleasure as we're going to have tonight. Because she's been staying at her dad's for two weeks, and we haven't had sex.

Two really long weeks.

I'm worked up now, so I dim the lights and join the girl in yards of white lace on the bed. She doesn't notice me removing the books around her until I snap closed the one she's reading from. She blinks at me a few times.

"Sorry, I'm being awkward again, aren't I?"

I shake my head. "I think you're hot when you're awkward."

"I just want to make sure we do everything the right way so we can get pregnant as soon as possible."

I push her onto her back. "I think we've got the basics figured out by now, nutmeg. And you've been off the pill for two weeks."

It's not difficult to tug her strapless gown down and off her tits, so I start there. Fuck, I missed these tits. They're perfect. Her berry nips are hard and ready for my mouth, so I suck them like a greedy bastard, alternating so neither one feels left out.

"I need a pillow for my hips if we do missionary style first."

"You don't need a pillow for your hips."

"But—"

"Megan, baby. We got this."

She nods. "I'm overthinking again. I can't help it. I'm not forcing you into this too soon, am I? I realize I get hyper-focused sometimes. But just because I want to start a family now doesn't mean you do. If you're not sure—"

"Are you kidding me right now? I am putting a baby inside you tonight."

She smiles. Ever since we decided to start trying to get her pregnant on our wedding night, I haven't thought about much else. I want everyone to see she belongs to me. I can't wait to see her with a big belly.

I am so turned on right now I'm leaking pre-come that I don't really want to waste. It's time to get my bride in the mood. And I'm really good at that. I tug her nipple with my teeth.

"First, I'm fucking that married pussy while you wear this wedding dress. I hope you didn't mean to keep it pretty because we are going to violate this lace, baby. It's going to be filthy and come stained." The color of her cheeks darken. She likes it when I talk dirty. The more dirty talk I give her, the wetter she gets.

I unzip my pants and pull my dick out. It's hard as fucking granite. I'm not going to last too long this round. Something about us having sex in these formal clothes makes it hot. Like it's some kind of taboo to take a girl in her wedding lace.

I bunch her skirt up. Garters. White lace stockings. No panties. That's my girl. "You're fucking perfect, Megan." Her pussy is glistening already. "You ready to take my married cock?"

She's thinking about pillows for her hips, I can tell. So I part those pretty lips with the head of my cock and slide in. She sucks in air when my balls hit her ass. I bet she can't get a full breath with that dress squeezing her rib cage. So I make it quick for us both, my thumb on her clit and my cock stroking her sweet spot, she comes and I follow.

Round One is in the books, but we have this suite for three days, and she's not getting out of bed for the next seventy-two hours.

Megan

AN HOUR LATER

I don't feel pregnant. I'm probably not. Not yet. I might not even get pregnant tonight. But ever since we decided to start trying on our wedding night, all I can think of is having Brody's baby.

So far, we haven't done the things the books say to do. Especially when he came in my mouth. That's certainly not going to achieve our goal. But that was my fault. I wanted him to. Sometimes I get a little greedy.

But Brody is right. We don't need to do this by the book. People get pregnant all the time without making a special effort.

"I can hear you thinking," Brody says into the dark.

"I thought you were sleeping."

"You were thinking too loud for me to sleep." He kisses me while he rolls me onto my back. He glides his kisses down my skin, stopping at my stomach. "I can't wait to see you round with my baby." He presses his cheek into my belly. "I love you so much, Megan. I didn't know I could ever feel like this. You are my whole life. I swear to God, I'll take care of you and our family. I'll always put you first."

I feel like his words are squeezing my heart. He's told me plenty about his dad, how he would spend all the money on booze and cigarettes and hit Brody and his mom. I know Brody thought he would never have a family because of the way he grew up. But then he met me and wanted to be the man his dad wasn't.

I hold him to me and am thankful for the dark that wraps around us like a shelter against the world. Brody and I are the most unlikely couple to ever fall in love. Neither of us believed we could be loved or love anyone else. Now we're married. Now we want a baby.

We're going to make one. Tonight. Now. I can feel it.

"Brody...I need...fill me," I whisper into the dark. "Please fill me up."

He lifts his head and catches my gaze in his. His gets dark. Very dark. Primal. He is wild. Untamable. Hungry.

"I'm going to breed you tonight, baby." He's on his knees now, lining up his cock, sliding it through my labia. "Your sugary cunt is getting my dick all wet. You're so damn wet." He slides into me easily. "That's it. I can feel you pulsing around me. Squeezing me. Your pussy is kneading my dick, baby. My balls are so heavy. They're ready to make you a mama. Fuck."

He moves over me, and I love the substantial weight of him on my body. But he's not moving like he usually does. The frantic, pounding dance we usually do. Instead, he barely rocks his hips at all. But I can feel his cock inside me. It's heavy and twitching. Growing.

"Slow, deep fuck. That's what you're getting now, babe." His voice is rough and weighted heavily with lust. His fingers bite into my hips. "Just let me stay in here, babe. Just like that. So good. So fucking good."

He moves my hands to either side of my head and our fingers entwine in a desperate grasp as he grinds his pelvis into me so maddeningly slow. His big body covers mine completely, and there is no world outside of our embrace. He fastens our mouths in a kiss unlike anything we've ever done before. Logic fails me as to why I feel a deeper level of intimacy in this moment, but I am consumed by our love.

Every muscle on his body is taut. It's killing him to hold back, to go so slow. It's heavenly torture. He's thickening inside me, a sensation I've never noticed before. I feel like I'm blooming deep inside. Like a flower opening to the sun. Opening to him. My husband.

"God, wife. Your pussy is grabbing me. So good. It's so tight and hot. I never want to leave it."

We do this for a long time. He sometimes buries his face in my neck, sometimes worships my breasts with his warm, moist mouth. I feel like I'm drowning now. I arch into him while he sucks on my breasts, grinding into him. I need to move like I need air. I need more friction. Just more.

But he's not giving more. Not yet. The heat coming off him promises raw, pounding sex underneath all this control. But I have to break that control first.

"Brody?"

"Yeah, Meg?"

He lifts his head and looks into my eyes. We are so in tune with each other right now.

"I love you."

"I love you, too."

"Brody?"

He huffs out a chuckle. "Yeah, Meg?"

"Give me a baby. Now. Right now. I can't wait any longer. Please, don't make me wait. I need you to come inside me."

His eyes lose focus and he growls. "Taking my time here, babe."

I shake my head. "I was made for this. For you to fuck me. To fill me."

"Oh Jesus." He is straining, trying to hold on. I don't talk dirty very often. "You make me lose my mind, honey."

I arch into him as much as I can. "Please put a baby in me, Brody."

Without warning, his hips buck hard, his body tensing as he slams his length into me in an instant, his hips grinding against mine. He surges hard, pounding, drilling. His power is an awesome thing. His thrusts bang the headboard against the wall, and I can barely hang on. "This what you wanted?" he growls.

"Yes!" Oh God, yes.

I'm drenched in sweat—mine and his—as his hips thrash into me. My head spins and I'm breathless. I lose my sense of self—of time even. I feel like I am on another plane of existence. I'm an animal now. Existing to take him as he pounds into me harder than we've ever done. The forceful impact and the wave of sensations I feel of him throbbing inside me, deep in my core like a second heartbeat, drive the sound from my lungs. When I climax, it's a violent string of orgasms that pulls him deeper. Harder.

He is unrestrained now. Mindless. Like all he knows is fucking. He plunges in hard and clutches me to him, frozen in a space of agony and pleasure. So much pleasure. "Take it all, Megan. Take all of me." He shudders over and over, and as he empties into me, I come around his cock again.

We lay in the dark and perfect silence for a long time. I keep him inside me, reluctant to be separated from him ever again. I thought I knew love already. I thought what we shared before tonight was as much as anyone could. But he keeps finding ways to crack my heart open more so he can fill it in with his love.

"Are we still alive?" he finally asks. "That was...wow."

"I enjoy being married so far."

He kisses my hair. "Wait until you're waddling around with my son and cursing me for making you so big."

"Or daughter."

"Oh man. I bet she'll be smart like you."

I can't wait to find out.

FILTHY SWEET, RIGHT? If you enjoyed *Nailed*, please consider leaving a review so other readers who love hot, blue collar heroes and nerdy, awkward heroines can find their next obsession.

[1]

---

1. https://www.bookbub.com/profile/brill-harper

IF YOU'RE TIRED OF billionaires, maybe you're ready for some real men. Dirty, hardworking, and good with their hands are the kind of heroes you'll find in the *Blue Collar Bad Boy Series*. These guys aren't cultured. They are hot *AF* alpha heroes who know how to take care of the slightly nerdy women they fall for. For reals, this series is more fun than you knew you were missing. And they don't need to be read in order.

So which blue collar bad boy will you choose next? They are all rough, raw, and surprisingly sweet.

Like...the roadhouse bouncer and the actuarial sciences student in *Bounced*[2].

Or...the carpenter and the Jeopardy! nerd in *Nailed*[3].

Perhaps...the oil rigger and the kindergarten teacher in *Drilled*[4].

Mayhap...the tow truck driver and the sorority uptown girl in *Wrecked*[5].

Surely...the brick layer hot single dad and the babysitter in *Laid*[6].

How about...a returning military hero and the wallflower at Christmas in *Tagged*[7]?

Or...the farmer who needs a wife and wants the curvy waitress in *Plowed*[8]?

Or...the hot rancher trying to convince the city girl to stay in *Bucked*[9]?

Maybe...the bomb squad cop and his pregnant neighbor? Did I mention she's a virgin? You read that right. Try *Banged*[10].

---

2.   *https://books2read.com/Bounced*

3.   *https://books2read.com/Nailed*

4.   *https://books2read.com/Drilled*

5.   *https://books2read.com/wrecked*

6.   *https://books2read.com/laid*

7.   *https://books2read.com/tagged*

8.   *https://books2read.com/plowed*

9.   *https://books2read.com/bucked*

10.   *https://books2read.com/banged*

And surely...the modern day Viking bartender and the bookworm virgin in *Tapped*[11]?

About the author

LIKE FIRST TIMES? FORBIDDEN fruit? *Yes, please.*

Love a hot, dominant alpha claiming what's his? *Fuck, yeah.*

Want to watch him fall hard for the sweetest fantasy he didn't know he needed? Me too!

I'm Brill Harper and I love happily ever afters, smokin' hot bad boys, and quirky, often nerdy, heroines that I'd love to be friends with off page. These ladies are not perfect—but they're perfect for one man—and he's always sexy AF.

Seriously—these heroes only have one weakness, and it's sticky, sweet love. They don't let anything stand in the way of taking what belongs to them. When it comes to the women they love, it's hard cocks, dirty talk, and soft, mushy heart feels.

*Brill is a sooper sekrit penname for a better known author who just can't handle all the dirty. She can't handle it...but can you?

BookBub[12]

---

11.   *https://books2read.com/Tapped-A-Blue-Collar-Bad-Boy-Book*

12.   https://www.bookbub.com/authors/brill-harper

Also by Brill Harper

Blue Collar Bad Boys
Bounced: A Blue Collar Bad Boys Book
Nailed: A Blue Collar Bad Boys Book
Drilled: A Blue Collar Bad Boys Book
Wrecked: A Blue Collar Bad Boys Book
Laid: A Blue Collar Bad Boys Book
Tagged: A Blue Collar Bad Boys Christmas
Plowed: A Blue Collar Bad Boys Book
Bucked: A Blue Collar Bad Boys Book
Banged: A Blue Collar Bad Boys Book
Tapped: A Blue Collar Bad Boy Book

It's Complicated
All Together
All at Once

Love in Brazen Bay
Wrong Number Text
The Right Stuff
So Wrong It's Right

Don't Get Me Wrong

Standalone
Dirty Jobs: a Blue Collar Bad Boys Collection
Notch on His Bedpost
Honeymoon With The Prince::A Modern Day Fairy Tale
Good Girl

Watch for more at https://brillharper.com.

www.ingramcontent.com/pod-product-compliance
Lightning Source LLC
Chambersburg PA
CBHW061440160726
47995CB00003B/971